MR. FUNNY'S
Red Nose Day

Roger Hargreaves

Original concept by
Roger Hargreaves

Written and illustrated by
Adam Hargreaves

Mr Funny is funny.

He sleeps in a boat-shaped bed in a teapot-shaped house, outside of which is parked his shoe-shaped car.

And all these things make people laugh.

And Mr Funny likes to make people laugh.

He is very good at it.

Or so he thought.

Until Mr Funny met Mr Grumpy.

Because Mr Grumpy did not laugh.

Mr Grumpy did not grin.

Mr Grumpy did not even smile.

Mr Funny pulled the funniest face he knew how to, a face he saved for special occasions, but not even a flicker of a smile appeared at the corners of Mr Grumpy's mouth.

Mr Funny invited Mr Grumpy for a drive in his shoe-shaped car.

Mr Funny had thought of just the place to take Mr Grumpy to cheer him up.

They drove to Nonsenseland.

Where they saw a dog out walking his pet worm.

Mr Grumpy did not smile.

Then they saw a giraffe wearing Wellington boots.

Mr Grumpy still did not smile.

They even saw a hippopotamus wearing
a spotty bow-tie.

The hippopotamus looked pleased with himself.

It was a very funny sight indeed.

Mr Grumpy sat, stony faced, in the back of the car.

Nothing he had seen had produced even a glimmer of a smile.

Mr Funny thought very hard and then he had another idea. He drove to his house. His teapot-shaped house.

"Wait here," said Mr Funny, and he popped into the kitchen.

He came back carrying a tea tray.

But Mr Grumpy did not notice this.

What he did notice was the size of Mr Funny's nose. It had grown!

Mr Grumpy's eyes opened wide. And for the first time in a very long time, Mr Grumpy's mouth did not turn down at the ends.

"Oh! I forgot the sugar bowl," said Mr Funny, going back into the kitchen.

When he came back, his nose was even bigger!

Mr Grumpy actually smiled.

"Oh! I forgot the teaspoons," said Mr Funny.

This time he returned wearing the largest, most ridiculous, quite preposterous red nose you have ever seen.

"That's ridiculous!" snorted Mr Grumpy.

"I know," giggled Mr Funny.

Then Mr Grumpy snorted again.

And the snort turned into a chuckle.

And the chuckle turned into a giggle.

And the giggle turned into a laugh.

And he laughed and he laughed until tears
rolled down his cheeks.

"That's the funniest thing I've ever seen!" laughed Mr Grumpy.

And then, Mr Funny fell over on his huge red nose.

And Mr Grumpy roared with laughter again.

He was laughing so hard he didn't hear Mr Funny's muffled voice . . .

"It's not funny. My nose is too heavy. I can't get up!"